Frédéric
Brrémaud

Federico
Bertolucci

Little TAILS

In the Savannah

with
Chipper & Squizzo

WRITTEN BY
FRÉDÉRIC BRRÉMAUD

ILLUSTRATED BY
FEDERICO BERTOLUCCI

TRANSLATION BY MIKE KENNEDY

LITTLE TAILS IN THE SAVANNAH (VOLUME 3)
FIRST PRINTING, 2017
ISBN: 978-1-942367-38-3

FIRST PUBLISHED IN FRANCE BY EDITIONS CLAIR DE LUNE

LITTLE TAILS IN THE SAVANNAH (VOLUME 3), PUBLISHED 2017, BY THE LION FORGE, LLC.
COPYRIGHT 2017 FRÉDÉRIC BRRÉMAUD AND FEDERICO BERTOLUCCI. ALL RIGHTS RESERVED.
LITTLE TAILS™ FRÉDÉRIC BRRÉMAUD AND FEDERICO BERTOLUCCI.
LION FORGE™, CUBHOUSE™, MAGNETIC™, MAGNETIC COLLECTION™, AND
THE ASSOCIATED DISTINCTIVE DESIGNS ARE TRADEMARKS OF THE LION FORGE, LLC.
PRINTED IN CHINA.
WWW.LIONFORGE.COM

Names: Brrémaud, Frédéric. | Bertolucci, Federico, illustrator. | Kennedy, Mike (Graphic novelist), translator.
Title: Little tails. Volume 3, In the savannah / written by Frédéric Brrémaud ; illustrated by Federico Bertolucci ; translation by Mike Kennedy.
Other Titles: Petites histoires de la savane. English | In the savannah | Little tails in the savannah
Description: [St. Louis, Missouri] : The Lion Forge, LLC, 2017. | Translation of: Les pétites histoires de la savane. | Interest age level: 5 and up. | Summary: In their cardboard box airplane, Chipper and Squizzo venture to the plains of Africa for a safari full of wild beasts of all shapes and sizes.
Identifiers: ISBN 978-1-942367-38-3
Subjects: LCSH: Puppies--Comic books, strips, etc. | Squirrels--Comic books, strips, etc. | Savanna animals--Africa--Comic books, strips, etc. | LCGFT: Graphic novels.
Classification: LCC PN6747.B77 L58313 2017 | DDC 741.5973 [Fic]--dc23

WAKE UP, CHIPPER!
IT'S TIME TO GO!

HNH?
GO WHERE...?

WE'RE GOING TO
AFRICA TO SAY HELLO
TO MY UNCLE BUZZ,
THE FLYING SQUIRREL!

OKAY!
UM, HOW DO
WE GET THERE?

BY PLANE,
OF COURSE!

YOUR CARDBOARD
AIRPLANE, YOU MEAN...
ARE YOU SURE IT
STILL WORKS?

OF COURSE!
IN FACT, WE'RE
ALREADY THERE!

AH, IT'S JUST A STUPID MONKEY...

HEH, YEAH...

...WHAT IS IT NOW? WHAT'S WRONG?

FRUSHHH

A BLACK MAMBA! ONE OF THE MOST POISONOUS SNAKES IN THE WORLD!

RUN!

FIIISSS

THAT WAS SCARY!

YEAH, WE SHOULD GIVE IT SOME SPACE...

...OKAY, I THINK WE'RE SAFE HERE.

HEY, LOOK! A BOAR!

NO, THAT'S A WARTHOG!

HE LOOKS SO WEIRD!

LET'S KEEP MOVING... I DON'T LIKE THE WAY HE'S LOOKING AT US!

BE CAREFUL IN THE TALL GRASS HERE!

WHY?

AHHH! M-M-MONSTERS!

HUH? NO, THAT'S A BABY GNU!

WHEN THEY'RE YOUNG, THEIR MOTHERS SEPARATE THEM FROM THE REST OF THE HERD...

...AND HIDE THEM IN THE TALL GRASS SO PREDATORS WON'T SEE THEM!

THEY STAY THERE UNTIL THEY'RE BIG ENOUGH TO RUN FAST!

...CHEETAHS USE THEIR SPEED TO CATCH THEIR PREY...

...THAT'S WHY THEY HUNIT IN THE DAY -- SO THEY CAN SEE WHERE THEY'RE GOING! ALSO...

...UM, WHERE'D YOU GET THAT BONE?

OH -- YOW!

STEALING A BONE FROM HYENAS... ARE YOU OUT OF YOUR MIND?!

BELIEVE ME, THEY ARE NASTY BEASTS!

WOAH -- SLOW DOWN!

A BUFFALO AND A RHINOCEROS...

THOSE TWO ANIMALS AREN'T VERY WELCOMING...

...WE SHOULD LEAVE QUIETLY!

WHY DON'T WE CROSS OVER THERE? THERE'S A CROSSWALK! I CAN SEE THE STRIPES!

WHAT? WHAT IS IT?

YOU DOGS ARE SUPPOSED TO HAVE GOOD EYESIGHT, BUT YOURS IS TERRIBLE. THOSE ARE ZEBRAS!

OH, SORRY, MY NOSE IS STUFFY, I COULDN'T SMELL THEM... I MIGHT HAVE A COLD...

AT SUNSET,
ALL OF THE ANIMALS
GATHER AT THE RIVER
TO DRINK...

...BOTH PREDATORS
AND PREY!

THAT'S NICE!

SO NOW HOW ARE
WE GOING TO CROSS
THE RIVER?

I CAN GIVE YOU A RIDE ACROSS, IF YOU'D LIKE!

AHHH!

?

A TURTLE!

REALLY? YOU CAN DO THAT FOR US?

SURE!

THANKS, BUDDY!

YEAH, BUT, ER... IT'S NOT VERY COMFORTABLE...

YOU'RE TELLING ME! OOF!

THANKS AGAIN!

SEE YA!

THAT TURTLE WAS NICE!

YEAH, BUT SO SLOW...

THE SUN HAS ALMOST DISAPPEARED!

HEY, UNCLE BUZZ! WE'RE DOWN HERE!

WHY, BY THE TREETOPS -- IT'S SQUIZZO! GOOD TO SEE YOU, NEPHEW!

HOW ARE YOU, UNCLE? STILL FLYING, I SEE!

YEP! ALWAYS!

MEET MY PAL, CHIPPER! CHIPPER, THIS IS MY UNCLE BUZZ!

HEY, CHIPPER!

HI!

...SO A SQUIRREL WHO CAN FLY. IF I HADN'T SEEN IT, I NEVER WOULD HAVE BELIEVED IT!

BUT NOW THAT I THINK ABOUT IT... HOW ARE WE GOING TO GET HOME? OUR AIRPLANE WAS DESTROYED!

HA HA, WELL I HAVE A SURPRISE FOR YOU...

LET ME INTRODUCE MOKO. HE'S OUR AEROSPACE ENGINEER!

?

HOWDY!

AND HE FIXED YOUR PLANE!

WOW!

THANKS, MOKO!

CHEETAH

THE CHEETAH IS THE FASTEST LAND ANIMAL ON EARTH. HE CAN RUN UP TO 65 MILES PER HOUR -- THAT'S AS FAST AS A CAR ON THE HIGHWAY!

THAT'S WHY THEY DON'T HUNT AT NIGHT -- RUNNING AT THOSE SPEEDS IN THE DARK CAN BE VERY DANGEROUS!

DON'T GET A SPEEDING TICKET!

OSTRICH

OSTRICHES WILL SWALLOW STONES THAT HELP GRIND UP THE FOOD IN THEIR STOMACH TO HELP DIGESTION. IT'S A REALLY SMART THING, SINCE THEY DON'T HAVE ANY TEETH!

ELEPHANT

IT'S NOT JUST A SILLY STORY -- THE LARGEST LAND ANIMAL REALLY IS AFRAID OF MICE! NOT THAT THE TINY CREATURES WILL BITE ITS TAIL OR PULL ITS GIANT EARS, BUT THAT THE LITTLE THINGS WILL CRAWL INSIDE THEIR BIG TRUNK! THAT WOULD BLOCK THEIR ABILITY TO BREATHE!

GIRAFFE

WHEN A GIRAFFE GIVES BIRTH TO A NEW BABY, SHE REMAINS STANDING. THIS MEANS THAT THE BABY GIRAFFE BEGINS LIFE BY FALLING NEARLY SIX FEET TO THE GROUND! OUCH! BUT AN HOUR LATER, IT CAN ALREADY STAND AND WALK TO FOLLOW ITS MOTHER THROUGH THE SAVANNAH.

HYENA

JUST LIKE VULTURES, HYENAS FEED ON DEAD ANIMALS. BUT BEWARE -- THEY ALSO HUNT LIVE PREY, TRAVELING IN PACKS! THEY WILL EAT ALL PARTS OF THEIR PREY, AND THEIR JAWS ARE SO POWERFUL THEY CAN BREAK BONES. IN FACT, THEY LIKE TO EAT BONES SO MUCH, SOMETIMES THEIR POO IS WHITE!

BABOON

BABOONS LIVE IN GROUPS UNDER THE PROTECTION OF A SINGLE MALE LEADER. THEY ARE OMNIVOROUS, WHICH MEANS THEY EAT A LITTLE BIT OF EVERYTHING: PLANTS, INSECTS, WORMS, EGGS, LIZARDS, RODENTS... AND EVEN SCORPIONS!

MMM, TASTY!

RHINOCEROS

ALTHOUGH ITS SKIN IS HARD AND THICK, THE RHINOCEROS SUFFERS FROM INSECTS. TO AVOID GETTING BUG BITES, THEY WILL ROLL AROUND IN THE MUD, WHICH WILL THEN DRY AND BECOME LIKE A LAYER OF ARMOR. IT MAY SEEM LIKE A DIRTY PRACTICE, BUT IT WORKS PRETTY WELL!

LION

UNLIKE OTHER BIG CATS, LIONS HUNT IN GROUPS. ACTUALLY, IT'S THE FEMALE LIONESSES WHO DO THE HUNTING, USUALLY IN THE EARLY MORNING OR AT NIGHTFALL. THE MALE LIONS SPEND MOST OF THE DAY SLEEPING AND PATROLLING THE AREA TO PROTECT THE PRIDE FROM THREATS AND OTHER STRANGE MALE LIONS WHO MIGHT CAUSE TROUBLE.

WOW... LIONS SLEEP BETWEEN 16 AND 20 HOURS A DAY!

I DON'T SEE WHAT'S SO INCREDIBLE ABOUT THAT... ZZZ...

I KNEW I HAD SOMETHING IN COMMON WITH THEM... ZZZ...